This book belongs to:

....

Sometimes Mimi and her friends fly all the way to our huge
world and have lots of fun tiptoeing into toyshops and playing
hide-and-seek in the dolls' houses. Before they fly home again,
they whisper their stories to Clare and Cally,
so now YOU can hear them too!

For dear Chloe – and for little Tinker too – Love from C.B.
For Helen, who was full of magic and light xx – C.J-I.

Hazel   Rose   Mimi   Acorn   Lily

First published 2015 by Macmillan Children's Books
an imprint of Pan Macmillan,
a division of Macmillan Publishers Limited
20 New Wharf Road, London N1 9RR
Associated companies throughout the world

www.panmacmillan.com

ISBN: 978-1-4472-7700-2
Text copyright © Clare Bevan 2015
Illustrations copyright © Cally Johnson-Isaacs 2015

1 3 5 7 9 8 6 4 2

A CIP catalogue record for this book is available from the British Library.

Printed in China

mimi's magical Fairy Friends

Freckle the Fairy Puppy

by Clare Bevan and Cally Johnson-Isaacs

MACMILLAN CHILDREN'S BOOKS

SWISH! SWOOP! A breeze was blowing and the sky was filled with excited fairies! Mimi and her friends were learning how to balance on the whirling wind.

"Look out, Rose!" called Mimi. "Don't bump into the birds."
"I wonder where the breeze will take us," Rose called back.

The wind had carried them all the way to Toadstool Town —
and the doorstep of the Starlight Shoe Shop.

In the window they saw silver slippers for frost fairies and tip-toe
trainers for tooth fairies.

"Look at those boots for cats," laughed Mimi. "They'd be far too big for my kitten."

But Hazel and Acorn were already next door, peering through the window of the Wishful Pet Shop.

"Oh!" cried Hazel, pointing at a tiny dragon who puffed blue smoke.
"I'd love her, but dragons grow *so* big. They need a cave. Or a castle."

WISHFUL PET SHOP

"I'd wish for a unicorn," said Rose softly.

But Acorn was already making a wish of her own:

"Bring me a puppy,
playful and true—
With spotty ears
and wings of blue."

YIP! YAP! FLAP! Out of the pet shop scampered a fairy puppy who sat at Acorn's feet and licked her fingers.
"Pets like to choose their owners," laughed the pet shop fairy.
"And Freckle has chosen YOU!"

Acorn hugged her new puppy. "But how much does he cost?" she asked.
"Three good deeds," said the pet shop fairy. "If you listen and look, you'll soon find a way to turn sadness into smiles."

So the fairies held hands and whispered together:

"Fountain and forest
and sunflower seeds,
Help us to gather
our three good deeds."

"Woof!" Freckle was tugging Acorn's wand.
"He's taking us to the fountain in Sparkle Park,"
said Mimi, as the puppy raced ahead.

Sparkle Fountain

He whizzed past a fairy godmother who was watching him with sad eyes.

"Look at him now!" cried Acorn. Freckle was dancing in the fountain on his two back paws.

Suddenly he jumped out of the water and gave himself a wriggly, jiggly shake.

SPLISH! SPLOSH!
Oh no! Now the poor fairy godmother was soaking wet, and she looked even more upset.

"Naughty Freckle!" the fairies gasped.
But the fairy godmother just shook her soggy skirt and began to *laugh*!

"That's the best fun I've had for a hundred years," she exclaimed.
"You've made me smile again. Thank you."

She gave Freckle a glittery collar and skipped happily away.

Acorn patted her puppy's head.
"You've turned sadness into a smile," she said.
"That's good deed number one."

Suddenly, Freckle stood still. He twitched his ears and his blue wings quivered.
"I think he's listening to a far-away sound," said Hazel.
"But that's the way to the Frightening Forest," groaned Rose.

Frightening Forest

"Let's follow him," cried Acorn bravely. "Off you go, Freckle!"
Away they all soared, towards the deep, dark woods.

Down they swooped . . .
to find a young elf weeping loudly. "I've walked too far and I'm lost,"
he wailed, as Freckle sniffed his pointy shoes.

"Don't worry," said Acorn, drying his tears. "My puppy has a clever nose.
He'll snuffle and sniff your footprints and we'll take you safely home."

"Woof!" barked Freckle, following a twisty pathway.

Round and round. Backwards and forwards.

Over and under, until . . .

. . . the fairies stepped into
a beautiful garden.
"I'm home! Thank you!" yelled the
elf, giving Freckle a shiny ball.

"Good deed number two," said Acorn,
as the puppy chased his new toy.

"Let's find my granddad," said the elf happily.
So the fairies played hide-and-seek between the sunflowers —
until Lily and Rose shouted, "Freckle! Stop!"

The puppy was digging holes *everywhere*, just as the elf's
granddad was waking up from his afternoon nap.

"What a mess! I'm very sorry," groaned Acorn. "My puppy did it."
"Thank you!" cried the elf's granddad. "I had *so* many holes to dig and I was terribly tired — but now I can plant my magic beans after all."

He gave Freckle a smooth stick and tickled the puppy's neck.
"Good deed number three!" cheered the fairies.
"Now Acorn can keep Freckle."

And they whizzed back to the Wishful Pet Shop on a friendly breeze.

When the pet shop fairy saw the glittery collar, the shiny ball and the smooth stick, he winked at Freckle and Acorn. "Three rewards for three good deeds," he murmured. "And one wish come true."

Then he waved his wand and a shower of magical sparks carried Acorn and Freckle quick-flick home.

When Acorn opened her door, she saw a fluffy towel for a wet puppy,
a bag of tasty food for a hungry puppy,
and a cosy basket for a tired puppy.

"Thank you, Pet Shop Fairy,"
whispered Acorn. Freckle wagged his
tail and snuggled up to sleep . . .

And that night he dreamed his best dream *ever*.